# Brian, My Pet Lion

## written by
## Jason Shapiro

## illustrated by
## Ayan Mansoori

TREE
MOUTH
BOOKS

Published by **TREE MOUTH Books**

treemouthbooks@gmail.com

Shapiro, Jason T.,  October 2020
    Brian, My Pet Lion  /  Jason T. Shapiro
    JUV002150     JUVENILE FICTION / Animals / Lions, Tigers, Leopards, etc.

ISBN: 9 781716 558702

Printed in the United States of America by Lulu.com.
1 2 3 4 5 6 7 8 9 10

Page design and layout by Peter Weisz Publishing, LLC
peter@peterweisz.com

# Special Thanks

This story was inspired by my son,
Ryan, and his cat, Roxie.

Today we picked up our new pet, a lion named Brian.

# On the way home, our lion rattled his cage to escape.
## THE CAR WAS SHAKING!

When we opened the front door to my house, the lion went flying like a lightning bolt. He knocked everything over!

I WAS PETRIFIED!

My dad picked up Brian.
THE SWEAT WAS DRIPPING DOWN MY FOREHEAD.

4

# He was ENORMOUS and had a FEROCIOUS growl.

ROOAAAARRRR!

Brian leapt high into the air and landed o our kitchen table. IT WAS TERRIFYING!

From under the couch, he grabbed my foot with his massive paw.
"HELP!" I screamed in fear.

ran across the house to escape, but Brian chased me up the stairs.
"SOMEONE, PLEASE STOP THIS CRAZY LION!"

Brian grabbed my favorite stuffed animal and tri
to rip it apart with his sharp, meat-eating teet

"BAD LION!" I scolded.

I raced through the hallway and climbed into my closet to hide! THIS WAS A TERRIBLE DAY!" I moaned.

Later that night, I walked into my sister's room. To my surprise, Brian was curled up sleeping on his lion bed. He looked so cute and peaceful.

My lion opened one eye and rolled over on his side. I kneeled down and carefully started to pet his back.

**B**rian started to lick my hand.
"That tickles!" I said with laughter.

14

rian's fur was so fluffy and soft.
It felt like cotton!

He started to purr really loudly. Like a lawnmower Brian then nuzzled his little head on my lap.

16

Suddenly, Brian seemed so much smaller. His growl sounded more like a MEOOOWWW.

Fierce, scary Brian was no longer a lion.

When I was calm and relaxed, so was my kitty cat, Brian. When I ran around scared and nervous, so did my lion.

19

The next time you're afraid and hav[e] your own Brian... Take a deep breat[h] and think of my cute little cat that wa[s] never a lion.

# Dedication

To Alyssa and Ryan:

I pray that when fear and uncertainty find you, that it is met with calmness and peace.

CPSIA information can be obtained
at www.ICGtesting.com
Printed in the USA
BVHW010544190122
626578BV00004B/52